From Country Roads to City Penthouses: The Journey of a Southern Boy

From Country Roads to City Penthouses: The Journey of a Southern Boy

Jeremy Sims

Published by Jeremy Sims, 2023.

This is a work of fiction. Similarities to real people, places, or events are entirely coincidental.

FROM COUNTRY ROADS TO CITY PENTHOUSES: THE JOURNEY OF A SOUTHERN BOY

First edition. September 19, 2023.

ISBN: 979-8223096207

Written by Jeremy Sims.

Also by Jeremy Sims

Awakened Wellness: Are YOU Spiritually Motivated Yet?
From Country Roads to City Penthouses: The Journey of a Southern
Boy
Good Leader Vs. Bad Leaders: A Roadmap to Authenticity

Chapter 1: Born on the Bayou

I was born among the magnolia trees and river bends of Mississippi, where the aroma of fried chicken and cornbread wafted through the air and the sound of cicadas sung the hymns of the evening. Life was simple. Our small wooden house was nestled on a quiet country road, surrounded by expansive fields and forests.

I was born among the magnolia trees and river bends of Mississippi, where the aroma of fried chicken and cornbread wafted through the air and the sound of cicadas sung the hymns of the evening. Life was simple. Our small wooden house was nestled on a quiet country road, surrounded by expansive fields and forests.

The heart of the South ran deep in our family. Generations had lived off this land, passing down tales of harvests, hardships, and happiness. My grandmother would often say, "We carry the spirit of the bayou within us," and I knew it to be true. The bayou wasn't just a landscape to us; it was a part of our very souls.

Every morning, as the sun peeked over the horizon, casting a golden hue upon the misty fields, I'd hear the familiar creak of the porch swing. My father would be there, sipping his black coffee, watching the world awaken. He was a proud man, with hands that bore the testimony of hard labor and eyes that twinkled with the wisdom of the ages.

Mama, on the other hand, was the very essence of warmth and love. She had a song for every occasion and a hug for every sorrow. The kitchen was her domain, and it was there that she spun magic. From her fried catfish to her peach cobbler, every dish was a testament to her love for us.

My younger sister, Clara, and I grew up playing amidst the reeds and chasing fireflies as dusk set in. We built rafts out of driftwood, pretending to be explorers charting unknown territories. The bayou was our playground, and every corner held a new adventure. The ancient oaks, with their moss-draped limbs, became fortresses, and the tadpole-filled ponds were mysterious worlds to be discovered.

On Sundays, we'd all dress up in our best and head to the little white church with small bricks down the lane. The gospel melodies, filled with passion and devotion, resonated deeply within me. It was there that the seed of spirituality, which would later become the compass of my life, was planted.

But like every Southern tale, ours was not without its shadows. While the days were filled with joy and laughter, the nights sometimes whispered secrets of long-forgotten sorrows. The old-timers spoke of Civil War battles, of love lost, and of times when life was a relentless struggle. These stories, told under the canopy of stars, gave me a profound appreciation for the resilience of the human spirit.

But like every Southern tale, mine too was painted with both light and shade. While my days were enveloped in the gentle embrace of nature and the love of my kin, nights had a different story to tell. As the golden hues of the setting sun gave way to the deep indigo of the night, shadows would emerge, both outside and within me.

My family home, passed down through generations, had walls that seemed to breathe with memories. The wooden floors creaked softly, echoing footsteps of those who walked before me. And sometimes, in the stillness of the night, I'd swear I could hear faint whispers, echoes of conversations long past.

There were nights when I'd lie in bed, the room illuminated only by the pale moonlight filtering through the gaps in the curtains, and I'd feel an inexplicable heaviness. It was as if the weight of generations, with their joys, sorrows, triumphs, and regrets, pressed down upon my chest. These were the moments when I felt deeply connected to the past, to the stories and souls that had shaped my lineage.

The elders, with their deep-set eyes and time-worn faces, were the keepers of these tales. On long summer evenings, when the air was thick with the scent of blooming jasmine, they'd gather us younger ones around a crackling fire. With each flicker of the flames, stories of our ancestors came alive.

I heard tales of brave men who fought in the Civil War, of the heartaches they endured and the sacrifices they made. Stories of great-aunts who, despite losing their loves to the horrors of war, stood tall, holding their families together with sheer grit and determination. And then there were the stories that spoke of life's everyday battles—of droughts that threatened to break the spirit of the strongest farmer, of financial hardships that tested the mettle of families, and of personal demons that everyone grappled with.

While these stories were often steeped in pain and loss, they also carried a beacon of hope. They were a testament to the resilience of those who came before me, a legacy of courage and perseverance. The shadows, though dark and deep, were always filled with light. And it was this interplay of darkness and luminosity that taught me life's most valuable lesson: that even amid despair, the human spirit has an uncanny ability to find hope, to rise, and to forge ahead.

As the years rolled on, the allure of the world beyond began to beckon. The tales of bustling cities, of opportunities and challenges, filled my dreams. The bayou had nurtured me, shaped me, but destiny had other plans. It was time to step out of the comforting embrace of the magnolias and cicadas and find my own path. Little did I know then, the journey would be filled with twists and turns, leading me from the familiar country roads to the dizzying heights of city penthouses.

Chapter 2: The Call of the City

The hustle and bustle of the city beckoned as I approached my twenties. The allure of bright lights and possibilities was irresistible. I moved to New York and soon found myself living in a penthouse, enjoying the wild nightlife, lavish parties, and the fast-paced lifestyle.

The transition from the quiet bayou to the concrete jungle was nothing short of overwhelming. The skyscrapers that pierced the sky, the never-ending hum of traffic, and the sheer magnitude of people – it was a sensory overload. Yet, in this chaos, I felt an inexplicable thrill. New York City was alive, pulsating with energy, ambition, and dreams.

When I first stepped onto the streets of Manhattan, it felt like I had been thrust into another world—a world far removed from the serene bayous and sprawling fields of Mississippi. My boots, which once tread on soft earth and dusty country roads, now clacked against unforgiving concrete.

Everywhere I looked, I was met with a sea of faces, each one telling its own story. There were people rushing to their destinations, their footsteps hurried, their faces set with determination. Street vendors called out, peddling their wares with gusto. The melodic honks of yellow taxis, the distant siren of an ambulance, the chatter of countless conversations—it was an orchestra of urban sounds, so different from the tranquil chirping of crickets and gentle rustle of leaves I was accustomed to.

And the lights! Oh, the lights. As night fell, the city transformed into a mesmerizing luminescent wonderland. Neon signs flashed, and billboards illuminated the streets with their vibrant glow. The city, it seemed, never slept, and neither did my sense of wonder.

But amidst this exhilaration, there were moments of intense vulnerability. The vastness of the city, both in its physical expanse and its cultural depth, often made me feel small, lost even. There were nights when the loneliness was palpable, and I'd find myself yearning for the familiar warmth of my hometown, for the comforting embrace of family and old friends. It was a paradox of emotions—feeling isolated in a city teeming with millions, yet simultaneously being intoxicated by its limitless possibilities.

I dove headfirst into city life. I tasted foods from every corner of the globe, from steaming dim sum in Chinatown to rich, savory kebabs in Queens. I danced the night away in underground jazz clubs, where the music seeped into my very soul. I walked for hours, exploring neighborhoods, each with its unique flavor and history. The city was a vast book, and with every day, I turned a new page, eager to uncover its secrets.

However, the city also had its sharp edges. The competitive spirit was relentless. Everyone seemed to be chasing something—fame, wealth, love, or merely survival. The pace was frenetic, and there were moments when it felt suffocating. Trust was a luxury, and genuine connections felt rare amidst the superficiality.

My first job was at a prestigious marketing firm in Manhattan. The position came with perks I hadn't even dared to dream of back in Mississippi: a swanky office with a view of the Empire State Building, luncheons at upscale restaurants, and invitations to the most exclusive events in town.

Shortly after, my life took a turn that felt straight out of a movie. The first time I stepped into my office, I was met with a vast expanse of polished mahogany and floor-to-ceiling windows that framed the iconic skyline of Manhattan. From my desk, the Empire State Building stood tall and proud, a constant reminder of the city's grandeur and the endless possibilities it held.

The wardrobe change was my first wake-up call. Gone were the days of casual cotton shirts and worn-out jeans. My closet quickly filled with tailored suits, silk ties, and polished leather shoes that clicked confidently against the marble floors of the company's hallways. Every morning, I'd don a crisp white shirt, adjust my tie in the reflection of the elevator's gleaming doors, and step out into the world of corporate New York.

Luncheons became an event in themselves. I dined at rooftop restaurants where the silverware gleamed and waiters moved with a choreographed grace. Places where you could taste the world on a plate - truffle-infused risottos, delicate sashimi, or rich duck confit that melted in your mouth. And the wines! Oh, the wines. I was introduced to vintages and bouquets I never knew existed, each bottle a story.

But it wasn't just about the food. These luncheons were where deals were made, alliances forged, and the future of brands decided. I quickly learned the art of conversation, how to navigate the undercurrents of corporate politics, and how to seal a deal with charm and a firm handshake.

The events, though, were the cherry on top. The first invitation I received was embossed in gold, summoning me to an art gala at a private Upper East Side mansion. The who's who of New York were in attendance, casually discussing million-dollar art acquisitions over champagne. Soon, my calendar was dotted with invites—movie premieres where I'd brush shoulders with celebrities, yacht parties with breathtaking views of the Statue of Liberty, and even a charity ball where I had the honor of sharing a dance with a renowned Broadway actress.

But perhaps the most unexpected perk was the network I built. I met people from all walks of life—CEOs, artists, tech moguls, and even diplomats. Conversations went beyond work, delving into dreams, passions, and shared visions for the future. It was a melting pot of brilliance and ambition, and I was right in the center of it.

YET, AMIDST ALL THESE luxuries, what I cherished the most were the moments of introspection. Late nights in my office, when the city lights twinkled below and the hum of traffic was a distant lullaby, I'd reflect on my journey—from the tranquil bayous of Mississippi to the pulsating heart of Manhattan. The perks, as grand as they were, were merely symbols of a larger transformation—a boy from the South, navigating and thriving in the big city.

It wasn't long before I met Ryan, a suave real estate mogul with a penchant for luxury. We hit it off instantly. He introduced me to the crème de la crème of New York society. From yacht parties to Broadway premieres, every night was a celebration of opulence and decadence.

Ryan and I were a striking contrast, yet it was perhaps these very differences that drew us together. While I hailed from the tranquil Mississippi delta with tales of sprawling cotton fields and folk music under starry skies, Ryan was a bona fide New Yorker, born into wealth, with the Empire State Building etched into his very DNA.

From the get-go, our bond was undeniable. Our first meeting was at a fundraiser held at The Metropolitan Museum of Art. Ryan, in a perfectly tailored tuxedo, approached me with a confident swagger and an outstretched hand, complimenting my decidedly Southern charm. We quickly found common ground talking about everything from world travels to our shared love for blues music.

He became my guide, my mentor in the labyrinthine world of New York's elite. With Ryan by my side, every door swung open, and I was ushered into the very heart of the city's glitterati.

The yacht parties were something out of a dream. Anchored against the backdrop of Manhattan's twinkling skyline, these colossal vessels were a testament to human luxury. Crystal chandeliers hung from decks, jazz bands serenaded guests, and waiters moved silently, offering glasses filled with the finest champagnes. Everyone who was anyone in New York was there – actors, politicians, business magnates. The conversations flowed as smoothly as the drinks, with deals being made and partnerships forged under the silvery moonlight.

Ryan and I also attended a myriad of Broadway premieres. The red carpet was our playground, where the flash of cameras never ceased, and fans clamored for autographs. Inside, the world's tales unfolded on stage, each performance an echo of the city's multifaceted character.

But it wasn't all glamorous. Some of the most unforgettable parties were the intimate gatherings in penthouse suites, where the city's intellectuals and artists congregated. Amidst walls adorned with avant-garde art, poets recited verses, musicians strummed melancholic tunes, and debates on world affairs stretched into the early hours.

Despite our whirlwind of social engagements, what grounded our friendship was the moments of genuine connection. Late-night drives through the city, impromptu dinners at hole-in-the-wall Italian bistros, or simply sharing stories of our past on Ryan's penthouse balcony, the city sprawling endlessly below us.

Ryan's gift to me on my birthday was the penthouse I'd soon call home. Perched on the 52nd floor of a glass tower, the apartment offered panoramic views of the city skyline. On clear nights, as I sipped on aged whiskey, the city lights would twinkle, mirroring the stars I once watched from my bayou porch.

But life in the fast lane was not all glitz and glamor. The high-stake deals, cutthroat competition, and the relentless pressure to keep up appearances were exhausting. The very same parties that once fascinated me began to feel superficial. Conversations were peppered with hidden agendas, and relationships were transactional.

Living life in the fast lane meant that every minute was accounted for, every second was precious. The city that never slept didn't allow its inhabitants much rest either. From early morning meetings to late-night soirees, my calendar was a mosaic of commitments, each one seemingly more important than the last.

Yet, behind the sheen of success and power, there were dark undercurrents. It soon became evident that in this world, trust was a luxury few could afford. At business dinners, beneath the clink of expensive wine glasses, deals were brokered with veiled threats and promises. Every handshake, every smile concealed a world of calculations. Who could offer more? Who held the cards? Who was merely a pawn in this high-stakes game?

The parties, though swathed in opulence, became a hunting ground for alliances. Introductions weren't made out of genuine interest but rather strategic advantage. Every laugh, every shared secret had a price tag. An invitation to an elite gathering was not just an evening of revelry; it was a ticket to ascend the social ladder, a platform to flaunt one's influence and connections.

And then there were the friendships, or what passed for them. In a world driven by ambition, relationships were often built on the shifting sands of convenience. Friends of today could easily become rivals of tomorrow. The same people who toasted to your success could whisper about your failures in hushed corridors. Loyalties were fickle, contingent on the ebb and flow of power and favor.

THE WOMEN AND MEN I met were often enigmas, presenting curated versions of themselves. Genuine vulnerability, genuine connection seemed like relics of a bygone era. The dance of courtship, too, was a series of transactions. Dates resembled business meetings, where backgrounds were vetted, and futures were negotiated. The question was not so much about compatibility as it was about mutual benefit.

There were moments, sitting in my penthouse overlooking the vast expanse of the city, when I felt profoundly alone. The weight of maintaining a facade, of constantly playing the game, bore down on me. The glimmering lights below, instead of being symbols of opportunity, felt like a maze trapping me in its convoluted web.

It was a world where vulnerability was seen as weakness, authenticity was a rare gem, and every move was a calculated step in the dance of ambition. The fast lane, with all its allure, came at a price – the risk of losing oneself in its dizzying whirl.

I began to miss the authenticity of my Southern roots—the genuine smiles, the warmth of tight-knit communities, and the tranquil evenings filled with the chorus of cicadas. The penthouse, despite its luxury, felt cold and isolating. The vast windows, instead of offering freedom, often felt like barriers separating me from reality.

Amidst the whirlwind of city life, I also started exploring New York's diverse neighborhoods. I was drawn to Greenwich Village, with its bohemian vibe, independent bookstores, and cozy cafes. I would often wander through Central Park, feeling a semblance of connection to nature, even if it was manicured and curated.

GREENWICH VILLAGE, or "The Village" as locals fondly called it, was a stark contrast to the towering skyscrapers and opulent penthouses that had become my new normal. The Village held a certain charm that reminded me of the simplicity of Mississippi, albeit with an urban twist. Here, the streets were lined with historic brownstones and tangled ivy, a labyrinth of creativity and rebellion against New York's mainstream.

What drew me initially was the art. The Village had been the home to many legendary artists, musicians, and writers over the years. Everywhere I looked, there was a canvas of history and culture. Jazz bars with their dim lights and soulful tunes pulled me into a world where music wasn't just heard but felt. I'd lose hours in The Blue Note, absorbing the rhythms and melodies of talented musicians pouring their heart and soul into every note.

Then there were the bookstores. Unlike the sprawling commercial outlets, these were intimate spaces, each holding tales of generations. I would spend hours in places like Strand, navigating through the labyrinth of shelves, feeling the textured spines, and diving into the worlds within the pages. The old-book scent that lingered in the air felt like a warm embrace, a comforting reminder of days when I'd read by the fireplace back home.

But beyond art and literature, it was the people of The Village that truly captivated me. The area was a melting pot of personalities - students debating philosophy, poets reciting verses on street corners, artists sketching the world around them, and activists championing for change.

Conversations here were raw, real, and unrestrained. No hidden agendas, just genuine human connection.

In The Village, I found a refuge. It became my haven, a place to escape when the superficiality of the high life became too much. I enrolled in a pottery class, giving form to clay and grounding myself in the process. On weekends, I'd sit in Washington Square Park, watching street performers, playing chess with locals, and sometimes just laying on the grass, letting the world pass by.

I even dabbled in writing, finding solace in penning down my thoughts at quiet cafes like Caffe Reggio or Joe's. The atmosphere, with its ambient chatter, light jazz, and the comforting aroma of freshly brewed coffee, was the perfect muse. Here, amidst the cozy corners and candle-lit tables, I started journaling my journey, from the Mississippi delta to the heart of New York.

Greenwich Village was more than just a neighborhood for me; it was a reminder that amidst the chaos and complexity of life, there were pockets of simplicity and authenticity, waiting to be discovered. And in those cobbled streets and historic haunts, I found pieces of myself I thought I had lost.

The juxtaposition of my life was stark. By day, I was the Southern boy turned city slicker, clinching deals and rubbing shoulders with elites. By night, I was the introspective wanderer, seeking solace in the city's quieter corners, grappling with a growing sense of displacement and longing.

One evening, after an exhausting day at the office, I found myself aimlessly wandering the streets of Manhattan. The city noises, usually a comforting backdrop, seemed jarring. Each honk, every shout, amplified my growing unease. I felt out of place, like a piece of driftwood carried far from its shore. I was lost amidst the teeming millions, yearning for something I couldn't quite name.

I found myself drawn to the Hudson River. There, looking at its vast expanse, I was reminded of the Mississippi River's gentle flow. A flood of memories washed over me — the soft murmur of the waters, the quiet serenity of the bayou, and the unhurried pace of life. I recalled my mother's voice, singing gospel songs as she hung laundry out to dry, and the tales my grandfather told under the starlit skies. The contrast between those memories and my current life was stark, and a profound sense of dislocation settled in.

As I walked alongside the river, I came across a street musician playing a soulful blues tune on his guitar. The raw, emotive notes seemed to mirror my inner turmoil. I sat down next to him, losing myself in the melancholic melody. When he finished playing, we struck up a conversation. His name was Eli, a Southern native like me, who'd journeyed to New York in pursuit of his music dreams. But, much like my own experience, he felt the city's pull had led him astray from his true calling.

Our conversation, so candid and deep, was a stark reminder of the genuine connections I missed. Eli spoke of his plans to return south and reconnect with his roots. He mentioned a retreat in the Smoky Mountains that focused on spiritual healing and self-discovery. On a whim, I decided to join him. It felt right, like a step towards finding the balance I so desperately sought.

The retreat was transformative. Nestled amidst the lush greenery, I was reintroduced to the rhythms of nature. Days were filled with meditation, introspective sessions, and long walks in the woods. The peace I felt there was profound, a far cry from the restless nights in my penthouse.

One evening, during a bonfire session, I had an epiphany. I realized that while the city had given me material success, it had taken away my soul's tranquility. The pursuit of external validation had overshadowed my inner voice, the essence of who I was. It was time to recalibrate, to realign my life's compass.

As the years passed, the allure of the city began to wane. The skyscrapers that once symbolized opportunities now felt like claustrophobic walls closing in. The penthouse, though a symbol of my success, became a gilded cage. It was evident; I was standing at a crossroads. The call of the bayou, the pull of my roots, and the spiritual void I felt would soon set me on a path I hadn't anticipated. The journey from the magnolia trees to the city lights was about to take an unexpected turn.

Chapter 3: The Double-Edged Sword

The city, though exhilarating, was not without its pitfalls. The disconnect from nature and my roots began to manifest in the form of restlessness. The more I immersed myself in the material world, the more I felt the void within.

Living in the heart of Manhattan, surrounded by wealth and luxury, I began to recognize the duality of my existence. While part of me reveled in the conveniences and the modern marvels of city life, another part craved the authenticity and simplicity of my childhood. It felt as though I was straddling two worlds, and it became increasingly challenging to reconcile the two.

Every day, I would wake up to a breathtaking view of the city skyline from my penthouse, yet, instead of feeling on top of the world, I often felt a growing detachment. The rhythmic sound of the city below — the honks, the distant chatter, the perpetual hum — was a stark contrast to the serene melodies of chirping birds and rustling leaves that I was accustomed to in Mississippi.

The streets of Manhattan were lined with posh boutiques, fine dining restaurants, and theaters showcasing the best of Broadway. On weekends, my calendar was packed with events — gallery openings, rooftop parties, and private screenings. On the surface, it was a dream come true. I was living a life many aspired for. My circle comprised the city's elite: investment bankers, fashionistas, tech moguls, and rising stars in the arts. Every night, champagne flowed, and we celebrated life atop the world's most energetic city. But when the music dimmed, and the conversations died down, a sense of hollowness crept in.

I remember a particular evening, after a lavish party at a colleague's loft in SoHo, I found myself wandering the streets alone. The city, which was always awake, felt oddly silent. The towering structures, which by day stood as symbols of might and prosperity, by night seemed cold and impersonal. I began to question what lay beneath the sheen. Were the smiles around me genuine, or were they masked facades? Was I truly happy, or was I merely caught in the riptide of societal expectations?

ONE SUNDAY AFTERNOON, in search of solace, I ventured into Central Park. I sought out the most secluded spot I could find and lay on the grass, allowing the sun to kiss my face. The gentle breeze took me back to the open fields of my hometown. It was a fleeting moment of connection, a brief respite from the overwhelming dissonance I felt.

The more time I spent in the city, the clearer the chasm between my past and present became. The values I grew up with — community, kinship, humility — seemed overshadowed by ambition, competition, and a relentless quest for more. While I had countless acquaintances in the city, genuine connections were few and far between. The conversations, while intellectually stimulating, often lacked depth and soul.

I yearned to be seen, not for my accolades or my address but for the southern boy who still found wonder in fireflies, who felt peace under the vast expanse of a starry sky, and who believed in the healing power of heartfelt conversations on a porch swing.

It was a daily struggle, a tug-of-war between the allure of the city and the call of my roots. I realized that while I could physically relocate to the heart of a bustling metropolis, the heart of the boy from Mississippi, with its deep-seated values and memories, could never truly leave the bayou behind.

Every morning, as I drew the blinds of my penthouse, the sprawling metropolis stretched out before me. But instead of feeling on top of the world, I often felt buried beneath its weight. The skyscrapers, once awe-inspiring, began to resemble steel giants, blocking out the nurturing touch of the sun and the vastness of the open sky.

THE ELEVATOR RIDES down from my penthouse became symbolic of my emotional descent. The deeper I delved into the city's offerings, the further I felt from my true self. The parties, which were initially a source of excitement, turned monotonous. The laughter, the clinking of glasses, the flash of cameras - it all began to feel like a rehearsed play, where I was an actor donning a mask, hiding the growing emptiness within.

I began to seek refuge in the various pleasures the city offered. High-end boutiques, gourmet restaurants, and opulent theaters became frequent haunts. But every purchase, every bite of the most exquisite cuisine, every standing ovation was but a fleeting moment of joy. The void within only seemed to deepen.

My friendships, too, underwent a transformation. The city had an uncanny ability to make one feel lonely in a crowd. The friendships that were once forged in the heat of ambition and revelry now seemed hollow. Deep conversations were replaced by superficial banter. True connections were rare, and trust became a luxury.

And then, there were the temptations. New York, with its pulsating nightlife, presented vices dressed as virtues. Late-night rendezvous, clandestine affairs, and the lure of substances became a means to escape reality, even if momentarily. While they promised euphoria, they left behind a trail of guilt and discontent.

One particularly chilly winter evening, as snowflakes danced against my penthouse windows, I found myself sitting by the fireplace. The flames, with their hypnotic dance, beckoned me to introspect. I realized that the material success I had achieved was but a double-edged sword. While it afforded luxuries, it came at the cost of my peace of mind.

Yearning for a sense of belonging and purpose, I began exploring avenues outside my comfort zone. The city, despite its pitfalls, was also a melting pot of cultures and ideologies. It was in this vast metropolis that I first came across meditation centers, yoga retreats, and spiritual workshops.

This newfound interest was met with skepticism by my peers. But for me, it was a beacon of hope, a potential bridge between the two worlds I inhabited. As I embarked on this inner journey, little did I know that it would take me from the heart of the city to the farthest corners of the globe, searching for a balm to heal the wounds of my soul.

Chapter 4: A Traveler at Heart

To fill the void, I began traveling. From the historic streets of Europe to the spiritual temples of Asia, I sought solace. Every destination revealed a part of me I never knew existed. My backpack was filled not just with essentials but with stories and experiences.

The first stamp in my passport was Paris. The romantic allure of the City of Lights seemed like the perfect place to begin my odyssey. As I strolled along the Seine, the Eiffel Tower looming majestically in the distance, I felt the weight of the city slowly lifting. The rich tapestry of history, art, and culture engulfed me. The cobblestone streets whispered tales of love, revolution, and resilience. In the city's embrace, I found a reflection of my own journey—a blend of light and shadow, passion and pain.

Every corner of Paris was a revelation. The quaint cafés with their petite tables on the sidewalks beckoned me to sit, sip on an espresso, and watch the world pass by. I marveled at the juxtaposition of the city's deep-rooted history and its vibrant present.

Visiting Montmartre, I traced the footsteps of the great artists who once called this neighborhood home. Van Gogh, Picasso, Dali — their spirits seemed to linger in the air, in the narrow alleyways, and the sunlit squares. The bohemian atmosphere was palpable, and I often found myself lost in thought, sketching the scenes before me or penning down verses inspired by the city's charm.

The art was everywhere—not just in the world-renowned museums like the Louvre or the Musée d'Orsay but in the streets, the bistros, the markets. Street musicians played haunting melodies on their violins, artists sketched portraits by the river, and poets recited their verses in dimly lit underground clubs.

One evening, at a hidden jazz club in the Latin Quarter, I met Isabelle, a Parisian who shared my passion for travel and soul-searching. With her, I explored parts of the city that were off the beaten path—the serene gardens of Albert Kahn, the bustling African market in the 18th arrondissement, and the intoxicating scent of rare perfumes in Saint Germain's boutiques. Our conversations, ranging from the mysteries of the universe to our favorite croissant spots in the city, added layers to my Parisian experience.

Yet, amidst the allure, there were moments of profound introspection. I remember standing before Notre Dame, its gothic spires piercing the sky, and feeling an overwhelming sense of reverence and melancholy. The cathedral, which had witnessed centuries of human triumphs and tragedies, seemed to mirror my own internal dichotomy. Here, in this ancient city, my quest for meaning deepened.

Each night, as I gazed out of my rented apartment's window, the shimmering lights of Paris lulled me into a contemplative trance. The Seine, with its gentle ebb and flow, mirrored the rhythm of life—constant yet ever-changing. Paris, in its timeless beauty, was teaching me about the impermanence of life and the importance of savoring every fleeting moment.

By the time I packed my bags to leave, Paris had left an indelible mark on my soul. The city had not just been a destination; it had been a companion, a muse, a mirror. It had shown me that amidst the chaos of life, beauty could always be found—it was simply a matter of perspective.

But it was in the rolling Tuscan hills of Italy where I felt a profound connection to the earth. The picturesque vineyards, the olive groves, and the rustic charm of the countryside rekindled memories of Mississippi. I spent my days learning about winemaking, relishing the region's culinary delights, and surrendering to the languid pace of life.

But it was in the rolling Tuscan hills of Italy where I felt a profound connection to the earth. The picturesque vineyards, the olive groves, and the rustic charm of the countryside rekindled memories of Mississippi. I spent my days learning about winemaking, relishing the region's culinary delights, and surrendering to the languid pace of life.

From Europe, my journey took me eastward to the spiritual heartland of Asia. India, with its kaleidoscope of colors, sounds, and scents, was both overwhelming and mesmerizing. I found solace in the serene Himalayan foothills, meditating alongside monks who taught me about detachment, mindfulness, and inner peace. The temples of Varanasi, pulsating with devotion, showed me the depth of human faith.

The Ganges, with its eternal flow, became a metaphor for life—ever-changing yet constant.

The cacophony of the bustling streets in Delhi contrasted sharply with the tranquility I found in the ashrams of Rishikesh. Every morning, I would join the locals and pilgrims for the Ganga Aarti, a ritualistic offering of lights to the holy river. The harmonious chants, the ringing bells, and the radiant flames dancing to the rhythm of the wind painted a surreal picture. Each evening, as I sat cross-legged on the ghats, I felt an inexplicable connection to the vast river and the millions of souls that sought solace in its waters.

My exploration led me to Jaipur, the Pink City, where grand palaces stood alongside humble abodes, narrating tales of valor and romance from a bygone era. The colorful bazaars, brimming with handicrafts, gemstones, and fabrics, were a treat for the senses. But it was in the small, hidden alleys where I discovered the real treasures—spontaneous conversations with locals, children playing traditional games, and artisans meticulously crafting masterpieces.

Next was Kerala, God's Own Country. Floating on a houseboat in the backwaters, I witnessed a slower pace of life. The mirrored waters reflected the lush, green coconut groves and paddy fields. Fishermen cast their nets, while women washed clothes on the banks, their melodic songs blending with the sounds of nature. The Ayurvedic treatments I experienced here were not just about physical healing but also about aligning the mind, body, and soul.

But it was in Dharamshala, home to the Tibetan government in exile, where my spiritual journey took a deeper turn. I attended lectures by Tibetan monks, discussing the teachings of Buddha and the importance of compassion. One day, I had the rare privilege of listening to the Dalai Lama. His words on kindness, love, and universal responsibility resonated deeply within me, leaving an indelible mark on my soul.

India, in all its diversity, taught me that spirituality is not just found in meditation or scriptures, but in the everyday moments, in the smiles of strangers, in the sharing of meals, and in the acceptance of the transient nature of life. As I boarded the plane for my next destination, I carried with me not just memories, but a heart enriched by myriad experiences, lessons, and connections.

Thailand introduced me to the magic of the monastic life. Waking up to the sound of temple bells, offering alms to saffron-robed monks, and exploring the intricate pagodas filled me with a sense of calm. The practice of Vipassana, a silent meditation retreat, was transformative. Ten days of introspection, silence, and discipline revealed layers of my psyche I had never confronted before.

Chiang Mai, with its blend of the ancient and modern, captured my heart instantly. The bustling night markets with their aromatic street food stalls, the golden temples perched atop hills, and the friendly locals made every day an adventure. On a suggestion from a fellow traveler, I enrolled in a traditional Thai cooking class, discovering the delicate balance of flavors that make Thai cuisine so captivating.

Venturing south, the turquoise waters of the Andaman Sea beckoned. The islands of Phuket and Koh Phi Phi were a haven for the soul. I found solace snorkeling among the vibrant coral reefs, where the underwater world seemed like an entirely different universe, teeming with life and color. The beaches, with their soft white sands and swaying palm trees, were the perfect backdrop for introspective evenings and reading.

But it was in the small village of Pai where I truly felt connected to the ethos of Thailand. The community there lived harmoniously with nature, cultivating rice paddies, and maintaining age-old traditions. I spent days learning about local crafts, participating in traditional dance sessions, and understanding the village's customs.

However, the true highlight was a three-day trek to a remote hill tribe. Guided by a local, our small group trekked through dense jungles, crossed streams, and climbed mountainous terrains. The tribe, untouched by modernity, welcomed us with open arms. Their lives, although seemingly simple, were rich in tradition, wisdom, and unity. Nights were spent around bonfires, sharing stories, songs, and learning about their ancestors' way of life.

Thailand also introduced me to the Buddhist philosophy of "Mai Pen Rai" which translates to "It's okay" or "Don't worry." It encapsulated the Thai attitude towards life—taking things in stride, embracing challenges, and finding joy in the little things. This philosophy, combined with the spiritual insights I gathered, reshaped my perspective.

As I left the Land of Smiles, I was imbued with a renewed sense of purpose and clarity. The juxtaposition of serene temples and bustling markets, the balance of the spiritual and the worldly, mirrored my own journey, reminding me that life is all about finding that delicate balance.

In the vastness of the Mongolian steppes, under the canvas of a billion stars, I found a deeper appreciation for the simple joys of life. Living with nomadic families, moving with the rhythms of nature, and experiencing the raw beauty of the wilderness was humbling. The echoes of my Southern roots resounded in the melodies of the horsehead fiddles and the stories told around campfires.

The vast open plains stretched endlessly, an ocean of golden grass, occasionally dotted with white gers (traditional Mongolian tents) and herds of grazing animals. The winds whispered ancient tales, while the skies painted a dance of colors at sunrise and sunset.

The nomads had a way of life that had remained largely unchanged for centuries. They moved with the seasons, herding their livestock and setting up their homes wherever the pastures were most fertile. Their lives were intertwined with the land, their animals, and the elements. It was a life of resilience, adaptability, and harmony.

During the day, I would help with the herding - trying, albeit clumsily, to keep up with the seasoned horsemen as they expertly managed their flocks of sheep and goats. The nights were for stories. As we sat around the fire, they would share legends of Genghis Khan, tales of epic battles, love stories set against the vast steppes, and folklore of spirits that roamed the wilds.

The cuisine was hearty and deeply tied to their way of life. Dishes like *khorkhog*, a mutton dish cooked with hot stones in a pot, and *buuz*, dumplings filled with meat, became instant favorites. Fermented mare's milk, or *airag*, became a daily drink, an acquired taste that grew on me.

A particularly poignant experience was the Naadam Festival. Rooted in the warrior traditions of the Mongols, the festival showcased the "Three Manly Games": wrestling, horse racing, and archery. The energy was palpable as the entire community came together, dressed in their traditional finery, celebrating their heritage with pride.

But, perhaps the most transformative experience was the silence. Away from the cacophony of city life and the relentless barrage of modern distractions, the stillness of the steppes was therapeutic. It offered a space for introspection, for connection, and for truly being present.

Despite the language barrier, the bonds I formed with the nomadic families were profound. Their generosity, warmth, and wisdom were lessons in human connection. They taught me the value of community, the richness of tradition, and the beauty of a life in sync with nature.

As I packed up to leave, with a heavy heart and a promise to return, I carried with me not just memories, but lessons that would shape my worldview. The Mongolian steppes, with their timeless beauty and noble inhabitants, were yet another reminder of the intricate tapestry of human experiences and the universality of our quest for meaning.

With each journey, I collected not just souvenirs but insights. The more I traveled, the clearer it became that the true journey was inward. Every mountain peak, every sacred temple, and every sun-kissed beach was but a mirror, reflecting the landscapes of my soul.

Yet, with all the adventures and revelations, a part of me yearned for something more. The diverse tapestry of cultures, religions, and philosophies had enriched me, but the spiritual void persisted. The nomadic lifestyle had its charms, but the anchor of home and the warmth of familiarity began to beckon.

While the world outside offered a myriad of experiences, it was the journey within, fueled by the external explorations, that paved the way for the true awakening that awaited me. The traveler in me had journeyed far and wide, but the most profound voyage was yet to begin—a voyage into the depths of faith and surrender.

Chapter 5: Holistic Discoveries

In my quest for inner peace, I explored holistic therapies, attending yoga retreats in Bali and meditating in Himalayan caves. Nature whispered to me once more, this time blending with the teachings of spiritual masters.

The lush, verdant landscapes of Bali became my sanctuary. Nestled between serene rice paddies and mystical temples, the yoga retreat I chose seemed like a haven of tranquility. From the very first day, I felt a profound connection. The island's unique blend of nature and spirituality was intoxicating. The gentle sway of palm trees, the symphony of the ocean waves, and the harmonious chants that reverberated during early morning rituals cast a spell on me.

Each day began with a session of pranayama, harnessing the life force that pervades everything. I learned to attune my breath to the rhythms of nature, to the ebb and flow of tides, and to the gentle rustling of leaves. The asanas, or physical postures, further deepened my bond with the earth. Every stretch, every bend, every pose was a celebration of the body's capabilities and a homage to the divine energy within.

But it wasn't just the yoga that transformed me. The Balinese philosophy of Tri Hita Karana, which emphasizes harmony with people, nature, and the spirit, resonated deeply. The local rituals, ceremonies, and offerings were daily reminders of this delicate balance. I became a regular at the local pura (temple), partaking in purification ceremonies where the holy waters cleansed more than just the body—they cleansed the soul.

From the tropical climes of Bali, my spiritual journey took me to the majestic Himalayas. Wrapped in their ageless embrace, I felt both humbled and elevated. These mighty peaks, which had witnessed eons, whispered secrets of endurance, strength, and surrender.

In a secluded cave, I met Guru Ananda, a yogi who had renounced the material world to meditate and seek enlightenment. Under his guidance, I delved deeper into meditation, transcending the realms of the physical, piercing the layers of consciousness. He introduced me to ancient scriptures, which spoke of cosmic energies, the interconnectedness of all beings, and the dance of creation and dissolution.

The teachings emphasized oneness—with the self, with others, and with the universe. I learned the importance of dharma, righteous living, and karma, the law of cause and effect. The Himalayan winds carried chants and mantras that seemed to vibrate at the very frequency of the cosmos. Meditating amidst this grandeur, time seemed to lose its meaning. Days turned into nights, and nights into days, in an endless cycle of self-discovery.

Nature, in all its manifestations, became my guru. The rhythmic patterns of the universe, from the migrations of birds to the blooming of flowers, taught me about cycles, change, and impermanence. The holistic therapies, combined with these timeless teachings, cultivated a sense of wholeness. I felt reborn, not just as a traveler or a seeker, but as a conduit of divine energy.

Yet, even amidst these revelations, there was an undercurrent of unrest. My spiritual pursuits had provided solace, but there was still a void, an unanswered call. The pull towards something greater, more profound, was undeniable. My holistic discoveries were just steppingstones towards a more profound surrender, a total immersion into the divine will.

Chapter 6: The Spiritual Warfare

Despite these enlightening experiences, shadows from my past and the hedonistic city life haunted me. A battle between my higher self and worldly desires raged within. There were nights when the cacophony of city sounds would be drowned out by the battle cries within my soul.

The tug-of-war was palpable. Every time I closed my eyes, memories of neon-lit nights, of intoxicated laughter, and of fleeting relationships flashed before me. These memories were in stark contrast to the peaceful, holistic experiences I had recently embraced. The old and the new worlds were colliding, creating a tempest in my mind.

The city's cacophony became an ever-present backdrop to my thoughts, challenging the serenity I had found in distant lands. Every honk of a taxi, every shout from a street vendor, seemed to mock the peaceful chants I'd heard in the temples. The concrete under my feet felt hard and unyielding, so unlike the soft sands and grassy plains I had walked upon. The towering skyscrapers blocked the horizon, reminding me of how trapped I felt.

In the heart of the city that never sleeps, insomnia became my constant companion. The serenity I had found in the vast Mongolian steppes, the tranquility of the Thai monasteries, and the poetic solitude of the Seine's banks seemed like distant dreams. My penthouse, with its panoramic views of the city, felt more like a watchtower from which I observed a world that I was increasingly feeling disconnected from.

And then there were the people. My so-called friends in the city seemed to have changed, or perhaps, I had. Our conversations, once stimulating, now felt superficial. Their concerns, ambitions, and desires no longer resonated with me. The parties, which I had once eagerly anticipated, now felt like choreographed dances of pretense and artifice.

I began to question everything. Was it the city that had changed, or was it me? Was the spiritual enlightenment I sought merely an escape, or had I genuinely outgrown the life I once adored? It was as though I was caught between two identities, struggling to recognize the man in the mirror.

In my solitary moments, I would often reflect on the teachings of the monks, the wisdom of the nomads, and the beauty of the simple life. They had all spoken, in different ways, about the impermanence of life, about the importance of living authentically and being true to oneself.

The chasm between my past and present was widening, and I knew I had to make a choice. The allure of the city, with its promises of fame, fortune, and pleasure, was undeniable. But the spiritual journey I had embarked upon had shown me a different way of being, a way that felt more genuine, more meaningful.

As the days turned into weeks, the inner conflict intensified. I yearned for clarity, for a sign that would guide my path. And then, one fateful evening, as I sat on my penthouse balcony overlooking the sprawling city below, a realization dawned upon me, setting the course for the next chapter of my life.

Some days, the pull of my past life felt overwhelming. The familiar allure of lavish parties, old friends, and the glitz of the penthouse beckoned. I'd find myself wandering the streets of New York, intoxicated by the city's energy. Old haunts would call out to me—bars where bartenders remembered my favorite drink, clubs where I was always on the VIP list, and restaurants where the finest cuisines awaited.

But every sip of champagne, every dance to the pulsating beats, and every flirtatious conversation felt hollow. The more I tried to recapture the magic of my old life, the more disillusioned I became. It was as if I was trying to fit a square peg into a round hole; my old life just didn't resonate with my newfound self.

SIMULTANEOUSLY, MY spiritual practices seemed to lose their luster. The yoga poses felt mechanical, the meditation sessions distracted, and the teachings distant. Doubts clouded my mind. Was this spiritual path truly for me? Or was it just another phase, another attempt to escape reality?

And with each rising sun, the question grew louder: "Who am I?"

The memories of monks' chants were replaced by the all-too-familiar sounds of subway trains and street performers. The solace I once found in the rhythmic breathing of my meditation was disrupted by the constant barrage of emails, meetings, and deadlines. The spiritual books that once held my rapt attention were now buried under piles of business reports and urban magazines.

One evening, after a particularly grueling day, I found myself walking aimlessly through the city streets. The neon lights seemed too harsh, the city noises grating. By chance, or perhaps fate, I found myself standing outside an old jazz club I used to frequent with Ryan. On a whim, I decided to step in.

The sultry tones of a saxophone greeted me, reminiscent of the warm Southern evenings of my youth. For the first time in what felt like an eternity, I let myself be immersed in the moment. The music, raw and genuine, spoke of heartbreaks, love, dreams, and despair. It was the authentic experience I had been yearning for.

Later, as I conversed with the musicians, I realized how they too had their own spiritual journeys, finding God in the notes they played and the melodies they created. Their dedication to their craft, their pursuit of genuine expression, resonated deeply with me.

The realization hit me like a ton of bricks. Spirituality wasn't limited to Himalayan retreats or Thai monasteries. It was here, in this city, in the heartbeats of its people, the stories they shared, the art they created. I didn't need to renounce the world to find my spiritual path. Instead, I needed to integrate the teachings I'd acquired on my travels with the life I was living.

And so, I began my quest anew, seeking spiritual experiences within the city's confines. I attended seminars on urban spirituality, sought out mentors who blended modern life with ancient wisdom, and redefined my own practices. Slowly but surely, I began to feel a connection again, finding God in the most unexpected of places.

Yet, the true test was still to come—a confrontation with my past and an alignment of my future. The journey was far from over.

It wasn't just an internal battle. Externally, too, the challenges mounted. Friends from my city life didn't understand my transformation. They mocked my spiritual endeavors, labeled them as "phases", and tempted me with the old thrills. Meanwhile, my new spiritual acquaintances often seemed too detached, too unworldly. I felt torn between two communities, belonging to neither.

It was during one of these tumultuous phases that I had a particularly vivid dream. I found myself on a battlefield, reminiscent of those medieval epics. On one side were warriors dressed in radiant armor, symbols of light and purity, representing my higher self and spiritual inclinations. On the opposite side were shadows, manifestations of my past, my fears, and my worldly desires.

BETWEEN THEM STOOD a colossal chasm, with the vast skies above echoing the clash of thunder and flashing streaks of lightning. The landscape around was a stark contrast—on one side, rolling green hills and serene rivers reminiscent of my Mississippi roots, and on the other, towering skyscrapers and chaotic city streets symbolizing my current urban existence.

The first to charge were the shadows. They moved with a ferocity and speed that was terrifying, their forms shape-shifting from memories of past regrets to faces of people I had wronged or been wronged by. They were armed with weapons made of my insecurities and mistakes, aiming straight for my heart.

The warriors of light, meanwhile, stood tall and steadfast. Their armor gleamed brilliantly under the tumultuous sky, emanating an aura of calm and resilience. They wielded shields embossed with symbols from my travels—Buddhist engravings, Tuscan vines, Mongolian motifs, and more. Each warrior represented a different lesson or realization I had acquired during my spiritual quest.

The battle was fierce, with neither side yielding. But amidst the chaos, a solitary figure appeared—a sage with a serene aura, untouched by the warfare around him. He approached me and whispered, "The real battle is not out here, but within. Embrace both sides, for they are part of you. Only in acceptance and surrender lies victory."

I awoke with a start, drenched in sweat. The dream's intensity was unsettling, but the sage's words reverberated within. It became clear that the path to true spirituality was not in renouncing one part of myself for another but in embracing the entirety of my being.

THE BATTLES CONTINUED, but with a new perspective. Instead of resisting my past, I began to accept and learn from it. Each shadow, each memory, had a lesson to impart. And rather than idolizing spirituality, I grounded it in reality, intertwining it with my daily life.

This internal warfare, intense and challenging, paved the way for my true spiritual awakening. It taught me that enlightenment wasn't an escape but a deep dive into the self, warts and all. The journey wasn't about reaching a destination but about understanding and embracing every twist and turn along the way. The real spiritual warfare was not about victory or defeat but about acceptance, growth, and evolution.

Chapter 7: Despair and Darkness

The warfare reached its peak, leading me into the darkest corners of my mind. I grappled with questions about my existence and purpose. The luxurious penthouse that once felt like a palace now seemed like a golden cage.

Each morning, the expansive view from my penthouse, which once inspired awe and gratitude, now felt suffocating. The sprawling skyline, which used to represent dreams and possibilities, had turned into a horizon of emptiness. Every skyscraper, with its impressive height and might, seemed to mock my own insignificance.

The city sounds that had once been a symphony of life and activity had become a cacophony of dissonance. The honking of taxis, the distant sirens, and the murmurs of the crowd below seemed louder and more intrusive.

The luxurious furniture and contemporary art that adorned my living space, once sources of pride and comfort, felt impersonal. These were mere objects, devoid of any real connection or meaning. The emptiness within was amplified by the vastness of the space around me.

Ryan would often come over, bringing with him the allure of old times. We'd sip on expensive wine, reminiscing about our wild nights out, but even in his company, I felt alone. Our conversations, which once flowed with excitement and future plans, became stilted, filled with forced laughter and awkward silences.

The elevator ride down from my penthouse became a daily descent into a maze of masked emotions and superficial interactions. The doorman's greeting felt rehearsed, the neighbor's smile seemed fleeting, and the bustling city, with its millions, felt devoid of genuine human connection.

I started to avoid the glitzy events and parties that once filled my calendar. Each invitation felt like a glaring reminder of the façade I had built around myself. The cocktails, the music, the glamorous crowd – it all seemed so alluring on the surface, but beneath the shimmer and sparkle, there was a hollowness. Conversations revolved around acquisitions, vacations, and the latest trends, but real, meaningful dialogue was rare.

In my moments of introspection, I realized that the city had given me everything I had dreamt of – success, wealth, and a lifestyle many coveted. Yet, it had taken away something precious – my sense of self, my inner peace, and the raw, unfiltered joy of simpler times.

The boy who had once marveled at fireflies in the Mississippi night now yearned for a glimpse of stars in the polluted city sky. The paradox was clear: In my quest for upward mobility, I had lost my grounding. The penthouse, high above the city, had become my ivory tower, isolating me from the world I once knew and the person I once was.

The weight of existential questions bore down on me, crushing my spirit. "Why am I here? What is the purpose of all this? Does anything even matter?" These questions played on a loop, with no answers in sight.

There were days when I would sit by the window, watching the world go by, feeling detached and isolated. The cacophonous sounds of the city, which once thrilled me, now felt jarring. Every honk, every shout, every buzz seemed to amplify my internal chaos.

I withdrew from society, turning down invitations and distancing myself from both old and new friends. The vibrant art scene, the cultural events, the city's heartbeat—all of it seemed trivial, almost superficial.

My spiritual practices, which had been my lifeline, seemed ineffective in pulling me out of this quagmire. Meditation sessions became agonizing, as my mind spiraled into darker thoughts. The teachings, mantras, and philosophies that once uplifted me now felt abstract and unreachable.

The world outside continued in its relentless pace, but for me, time seemed to stand still. The nights were the hardest. The penthouse, with all its opulence, echoed with loneliness. The vast living space seemed to grow larger, the walls closing in, amplifying my desolation. The silence was deafening, broken only by the rhythmic ticking of the antique grandfather clock.

One fateful night, as I lay on the plush couch, drowning in my sorrows and lost in thoughts of despair, a violent storm raged outside. The fierce winds howled, and torrents of rain lashed against the windows. Nature seemed to mirror my internal tumult. But as hours passed and the storm intensified, I began to sense a strange solace in its fury. There was a raw, unbridled energy in the tempest, an untamed force that resonated with my restless spirit.

And then, as dawn broke and the first rays of sun pierced the dark clouds, a realization dawned on me. Just like the storm outside, this phase of despair was not permanent. It was a necessary catharsis, a cleansing of my soul. The darkness was not there to engulf me but to highlight the impending light.

With this newfound understanding, I slowly began to pick up the pieces. Instead of resisting the darkness, I embraced it, allowing it to reveal the parts of me that needed healing. It was a journey of self-compassion, of understanding that it's okay to be vulnerable, to break, to rebuild.

This phase of despair, while harrowing, paved the way for a deeper connection with the divine, a bond that wasn't built on rituals or practices but on raw, unfiltered emotions. It set the stage for the most profound chapter of my spiritual journey—a total surrender to the divine.

Chapter 8: The Divine Intervention

Amid this turmoil, a chance encounter with an old friend from Mississippi led me to a small church service in Harlem. The preacher's words touched my heart as if they were meant for me. It was there that I felt God's call.

Harlem, with its rich history of resilience and rebirth, seemed an unlikely place for my spiritual reawakening. But as I stepped into that quaint, dimly-lit church on a Sunday morning, an inexplicable warmth enveloped me. The wooden pews were worn out from years of use, the stained-glass windows depicted stories of faith, and the air was thick with anticipation.

The congregation, a mix of young and old, greeted each other with genuine smiles and heartfelt embraces. It was a stark contrast to the aloof interactions I had become accustomed to in the heart of Manhattan. There was a palpable sense of community, of shared experiences and collective hope.

The walls of the church, though faded and chipped, seemed to tell stories of their own. They had witnessed decades of sermons, baptisms, weddings, and funerals. They bore silent testimony to the struggles and triumphs of the Harlem Renaissance, the Civil Rights Movement, and the changing socio-cultural landscape of New York.

My friend, Elijah, with his ever-contagious enthusiasm, had spoken highly of this service. "There's something magical about this place," he had whispered as we entered. I looked around, skeptical yet curious, as the congregation started humming a soft hymn.

As the choir began their hymns, their voices rose in a harmonious blend of soul, gospel, and blues. Each note seemed to resonate deep within, awakening dormant emotions. Tears welled up in my eyes, not from sadness, but from a profound sense of belonging. I felt as though I had been led here, to this very place, to find solace and healing.

THE PREACHER, AN ELDERLY gentleman with a deep baritone voice, began his sermon. His words were simple yet profound, weaving tales from the scriptures with anecdotes from everyday life. He spoke of love, forgiveness, redemption, and the eternal battle between light and darkness. As he delved into the parable of the prodigal son, I couldn't help but see parallels with my own journey.

Midway through the service, a time for testimonies was announced. One by one, individuals stood up to share their personal stories of transformation, challenges, and divine interventions. Their narratives, raw and real, painted a vivid tapestry of human experience. It was evident that this church was not just a place of worship but a sanctuary of hope, where souls, battered by life's storms, came to find refuge.

As the service concluded, and the congregation poured out into the sunny streets of Harlem, I felt lighter, more centered. The weight of my past mistakes, regrets, and internal battles seemed less daunting. The church had provided a momentary reprieve, a glimpse into a world of faith and unconditional love. And in that sacred space, amidst the echoes of hymns and prayers, I had found a glimmer of hope for my own redemption.

After the service, I approached the preacher, my heart heavy with emotions. He looked at me with a knowing smile, as if he had been expecting me. "Young man," he said softly, "God has been waiting for you. All your journeys, your quests, your battles were leading you to this very moment. Surrender to His will, and you will find the peace you've been seeking."

In the ensuing weeks, that small church in Harlem became my refuge. I immersed myself in its teachings, in Bible studies, in prayer groups. The congregation welcomed me with open arms, and the sense of community was overwhelming.

The void that had consumed me began to fill with God's grace. My spiritual practices from the past were not discarded but integrated, giving me a holistic approach to faith. Meditation became a conversation with God, yoga a celebration of His creation, and my travels a testament to His wonders.

But it was in surrendering, in truly giving myself over to a higher power, that I found my purpose. My penthouse, once a symbol of despair, was transformed into a sanctuary—a place of prayer, reflection, and growth.

From the country roads of Mississippi to the bustling streets of New York, from the serene temples of Bali to the mighty Himalayas, my journey had been a tapestry of experiences, challenges, and revelations. But it was in Harlem, amidst gospel songs and heartfelt sermons, that I truly found my way home—back to God.

Chapter 9: Surrendering to the Almighty

With tears streaming down, I surrendered my all to God. The weight of worldly desires, regrets, and fears lifted. I felt a profound sense of purpose and belonging. I realized the city and its penthouses were not my true home; my true dwelling was in God's embrace.

The days that followed my surrender were transformative. Each morning, as the sun streamed through the windows of my penthouse, I no longer saw the looming skyscrapers or the chaotic streets below. Instead, I witnessed God's handiwork in every ray of light, every gust of wind, and in the distant hum of the city awakening.

The mundane tasks of daily life, which once felt like burdens, became opportunities for mindfulness and gratitude. The act of brewing coffee, listening to the birds chirp, or even reading a book, took on a new dimension. Each moment was a reminder of God's pervasive presence and the intricate tapestry of existence He had woven.

In my surrender, I found freedom. The relentless pursuit of material success, the constant need for validation, the thirst for the next big thrill—all of it seemed trivial in the face of God's infinite love. For the first time in years, I slept peacefully, no longer tormented by the questions that had once consumed me.

Conversations, too, underwent a shift. The superficial chatter that dominated most interactions was replaced by deeper, more meaningful exchanges. I began to listen more intently, not just to the words spoken, but to the emotions and stories they conveyed. It felt as though a veil had been lifted, revealing the interconnectedness of all beings.

The city, with all its noise and distractions, took on a new meaning. I walked its streets with a renewed sense of purpose, seeing God's presence in every face, every gesture, every moment. The once overwhelming pace of New York now felt like a symphony, each element playing its part in the grand orchestration of life.

The penthouse, though still opulent and grand, became more than just a space to reside. It transformed into a sanctuary—a place to commune with God, to study His word, and to grow spiritually. The lavish parties and late-night soirees were replaced with prayer meetings, Bible studies, and moments of quiet reflection.

My friendships evolved too. While I still cherished the bonds formed over years of city life, I now sought out connections that nourished my soul. Conversations shifted from the latest trends and gossip to discussions about faith, purpose, and God's plans for us.

But perhaps the most profound change was in my heart. I found an unshakable peace that wasn't dependent on external circumstances. Challenges still arose, as they do in life, but they were met with faith and trust in God's wisdom.

Weekends were no longer about exclusive parties or luxurious escapades. Instead, I sought out spaces of stillness and reflection. Parks became sanctuaries, where I would meditate or engage in contemplative walks. The church in Harlem became a regular destination, not just on Sundays, but whenever my spirit sought nourishment.

And perhaps the most profound change was in my relationships. Connections that were once transactional and fleeting transformed into bonds of genuine care and concern. I found myself drawn to individuals who, like me, were on a quest for a deeper understanding of life. Together, we would share insights, question old beliefs, and support one another in our spiritual growth.

The penthouse, once a symbol of my worldly success, was now a space of introspection and spiritual recharging. I began to host small gatherings, bringing together thinkers, artists, and seekers. We would discuss philosophy, share personal stories, and engage in collective prayer. These sessions became oases of enlightenment, offering respite from the desert of materialism.

I also felt an overwhelming urge to give back—to serve God by serving His creation. I became involved in community outreach programs in Harlem, helping those less fortunate, spreading God's message of hope and love. The blessings I had received, both material and spiritual, were now being used to uplift others.

People often asked if I missed my old life—the wild nights, the adrenaline, the unchecked hedonism. And while there were moments of nostalgia, they were fleeting. For in surrendering to the Almighty, I had found a joy and contentment that no city thrill could ever provide.

Looking back, it was clear that every step of my journey, every high and low, was divinely orchestrated. From the serene bayous of Mississippi to the pulsating heart of New York, from the sacred temples of Asia to the humble church in Harlem, each chapter was a steppingstone, leading me to the ultimate truth—that in surrendering to God, we truly find ourselves.

In surrendering, I had not lost my identity or my place in the world. Instead, I had discovered a richer, fuller version of myself. A self that was in harmony with the universe, anchored in faith, and driven by a divine purpose. The journey had come full circle – from the magnolia-scented air of Mississippi to the skyscraper-dominated skyline of New York, and finally, to the very core of my being.

Chapter 10: The Awakening

I sold my penthouse and founded a community center in the heart of New York, blending my love for holistic therapies and spirituality. Every day, I witness the transformative power of faith and healing, as city dwellers, just like the boy from Mississippi, find their way back home.

The community center, aptly named "Awakening," became an oasis amidst the concrete jungle of New York. Located in the heart of SoHo, the center was strategically positioned to attract both the weary professionals seeking a momentary reprieve and the artists and free spirits of the neighborhood hungry for deeper connections. The area, historically a hotbed for art and self-expression, seemed like the perfect location for a place dedicated to introspection and communal growth. Its facade, crafted with reclaimed wood and draped in climbing ivy, stood in stark contrast to the steel and glass skyscrapers surrounding it. Large windows invited in natural light, and a rooftop garden offered a serene escape from the chaos below.

Inside, "Awakening" was a harmonious blend of minimalist design and earthy comfort. The walls were adorned with art from local artists, showcasing a dynamic fusion of the city's cultural diversity and spiritual essence. Bookshelves were lined with literature spanning various traditions, philosophies, and wisdom teachings, inviting visitors to dive deep into the vast oceans of knowledge.

The center buzzed with activity. Morning yoga sessions commenced with sun salutations, honoring the dawn of a new day. Meditation rooms, filled with the scent of burning sage and calming lavender, offered solace to the weary. Workshops on holistic health, organic gardening, and spiritual studies drew people from all walks of life, united in their quest for a deeper connection.

The name "Awakening" was not a random choice. For me, it symbolized a reawakening of the soul, a rekindling of the spirit's eternal flame, overshadowed by the hustle of city life. This center was a manifestation of my own personal transformation – from the dazzle of material success to the luminous path of spiritual fulfillment.

One corner of the center was dedicated to the "Mississippi Nook." Here, I paid homage to my roots. Walls adorned with pictures of magnolia trees, bayous, and dirt roads, and shelves stocked with southern literature and comfort food recipes. It was a reminder of the simplicity and warmth of my childhood, juxtaposed against the backdrop of the bustling city.

Yet, the true heart of "Awakening" was its chapel. The idea for the chapel arose from a deep-seated desire to create a sanctuary within the center—a place where visitors could reconnect with the divine, irrespective of their religious or spiritual backgrounds. It was a homage to the universality of the human quest for understanding, meaning, and connection.

Walking into the chapel, one would first notice the quietude. The distant sounds of the bustling city seemed to fade, replaced by a deep, comforting silence. The air was imbued with a subtle scent of sandalwood and frankincense, an aromatic testament to my time in India. This fragrance, subtle yet profound, served to anchor visitors in the present moment, inviting them into a space of introspection and peace.

Above the altar hung a tapestry I had acquired from a Thai monastery. It depicted a Bodhi tree, under which sat a meditating figure—reminiscent of the Buddha achieving enlightenment. The tapestry, with its intricate embroidery and vibrant hues, encapsulated the transformative power of silent contemplation, a lesson I had learned during my Vipassana retreat.

Flanking the sides of the chapel were prayer wheels, an ode to my time in the Himalayas. Each wheel was inscribed with mantras in ancient script, and as they were turned, they symbolically sent blessings and prayers into the universe. Visitors often found solace in this simple act, feeling a part of something larger than themselves.

On the right side of the chapel stood a small statue of the Virgin Mary, a tribute to my Christian roots and the church in Harlem that had played such a pivotal role in my spiritual reawakening. Adjacent to it was a shelf holding sacred texts from various traditions—The Bible, The Quran, The Bhagavad Gita, The Tao Te Ching, and more. It was a testament to the center's commitment to interfaith dialogue and understanding.

The chapel's floor was laid with tiles that I had personally chosen during my visit to Italy. Each tile, hand-painted with care, narrated tales of love, faith, and the inexorable dance of life. They were cool to the touch, grounding those who walked upon them, reminding them of the earth's nurturing embrace.

At the center of it all was a simple wooden podium, from which spiritual leaders, thinkers, and members of the community shared their insights, experiences, and hopes. It was here that the essence of "Awakening" truly came alive—as people from diverse backgrounds discovered common threads in their spiritual tapestries.

In essence, the chapel was not just a place of worship but a living mosaic of my spiritual journey. Every element, every artifact, told a story, echoing the lessons, the challenges, and the epiphanies of a soul in search of its true home.

WITH THE ESTABLISHMENT of "Awakening," my days took on a new rhythm. No longer fueled by the relentless pursuit of success, each moment was now driven by purpose. I found immense joy in guiding others, sharing the wisdom I had gleaned from my own journey, and witnessing their personal transformations.

Stories of redemption became commonplace. A Wall Street executive, burnt out from the pressures of his job, discovered peace through guided meditation. A young artist, lost in the labyrinth of self-doubt, rekindled her passion after attending a spiritual workshop. A troubled teenager, teetering on the edge of despair, found hope and direction through mentorship.

As months turned into years, "Awakening" became a beacon of hope in New York. People, regardless of their background, age, or beliefs, flocked to the center seeking refuge, guidance, and community. The testimonials of changed lives, of renewed purpose, and unwavering faith, were a testament to the center's impact.

One evening, as I stood on the rooftop garden, overlooking the city lights and listening to the distant hum of traffic, a profound sense of gratitude washed over me. The boy from Mississippi, once lost amidst the allure of penthouses and city lights, had found his true calling. Not just in serving God, but in guiding others to find their own path back home.

The journey had come full circle. From the bayous to the penthouses, from despair to faith, the awakening was now complete. And in this newfound clarity, one truth stood out—the divine was not found in grand gestures or epic quests, but in the simple act of surrender, and in guiding others to discover the same.

Epilogue

From the serene country roads of Mississippi to the dizzying heights of city penthouses, my journey has been one of discovery, despair, and divine intervention. Through it all, I've come to understand that no matter where we are, it's our connection to the Divine that truly guides our path.

As I sit on the porch of my childhood home, the gentle hum of cicadas accompanying the setting sun, I'm reminded of life's cyclical nature. It's been years since I founded "Awakening," and yet, the essence of my journey feels as fresh as the day it began.

Mississippi, with its vast fields and tranquil waters, instilled in me the first lessons of spirituality. It was here, among the rustling leaves and moonlit nights, that I first felt the stirrings of something greater, a force that bound everything in harmonious unity.

New York, with its unyielding pace and glaring contrasts, was both a test and a teacher. In its maze-like streets and towering skyscrapers, I experienced the heights of worldly success and the depths of spiritual longing. It was a playground and a battlefield, pushing me to the very limits of my understanding, only to reveal the boundless expanse of divine love.

The experiences, the people I met, the lessons learned—each formed a chapter in the book of my life. A book that, in many ways, is still being written.

"Awakening" was my humble attempt to pay forward the grace I'd received. And while it began as a space of healing for others, it became a daily reminder for me. A reminder of the transformative power of surrender, of the beauty in every soul's journey, and of the omnipresent hand of the Divine guiding us at every step.

Today, as I reflect on the tapestry of my life, one truth resonates above all: our external surroundings, be they the tranquil bayous or bustling cities, are mere reflections of our inner state. It's not the destination, but the journey and the connection to the Divine within that truly matter.

In the end, all roads, whether they lead through dense forests, across vast deserts, or amidst neon-lit streets, converge towards the same eternal truth—the infinite love and grace of the Divine. And it is in recognizing this truth, in embracing it wholeheartedly, that we find our true home.

Don't miss out!

Visit the website below and you can sign up to receive emails whenever Jeremy Sims publishes a new book. There's no charge and no obligation.

https://books2read.com/r/B-A-AZLAB-PZIOC

BOOKS 2 READ

Connecting independent readers to independent writers.

Did you love *From Country Roads to City Penthouses: The Journey of a Southern Boy*? Then you should read *Good Leader Vs. Bad Leaders: A Roadmap to Authenticity*[1] by Jeremy Sims!

[2]

Authentic leadership is not something that can be developed overnight. It's a journey of self-discovery, growth, and continuous improvement. Here are a few key points to keep in mind as you embark on this journey: Self-Awareness: Authentic leadership begins with self-awareness. It's important to understand your values, strengths, weaknesses, and the impact you have on others. This self-awareness often deepens over time as you gain more experience and insight into your own behavior.Consistency: Authenticity involves being true to your values and principles consistently, regardless of the situation or pressure you may face. This level of consistency can take time to develop as you refine

---

1. https://books2read.com/u/mllQKv

2. https://books2read.com/u/mllQKv

your leadership style and align it with your core beliefs.Building Trust: Authentic leaders build trust with their teams and colleagues through transparency, honesty, and reliability. Trust is something that is built gradually and can take time to establish.Learning from Experience: Authentic leaders often learn from their experiences, both successes and failures. Over time, you'll accumulate a wealth of experiences that shape your leadership style and decision-making.Seeking Feedback: Continuously seeking feedback from others and being open to constructive criticism is a hallmark of authentic leadership. This feedback helps you refine your approach and adapt over time.Resilience: Authentic leaders often exhibit resilience in the face of challenges and setbacks. This resilience is built through a series of experiences that test your resolve and determination.Mentorship and Learning: Learning from mentors and leaders who exemplify authenticity can accelerate your own development as an authentic leader. Seek out mentors who can provide guidance and share their experiences.

Remember that authenticity is a journey, not a destination. It's a process of self-discovery and growth that unfolds over time. Embrace this journey, stay committed to your values, and continue striving to lead in a way that is true to yourself. Your authenticity as a leader will not only inspire others but also contribute to your long-term success as a leader.

Also by Jeremy Sims

Awakened Wellness: Are YOU Spiritually Motivated Yet?
From Country Roads to City Penthouses: The Journey of a Southern Boy
Good Leader Vs. Bad Leaders: A Roadmap to Authenticity

www.ingramcontent.com/pod-product-compliance
Lightning Source LLC
Chambersburg PA
CBHW031636170726
47990CB00017B/1310